To Betty
Love, light, joy,

aka Rattlin Cochise,
Santa Fe March 11/02

A BULLDOG'S GUIDE TO SMALL ENGINE REPAIR

Portlin Cochise

Woodley & Watts
MONTREAL · SEDONA · TAOS

A *BULLDOG'S GUIDE TO SMALL ENGINE REPAIR*

Portlin Cochise

The author gratefully thanks Danielle Leblanc, André Dussault, Milena Katz and Madeleine Partous for their generous help.

WOODLEY & WATTS
PO BOX 1783, SEDONA, AZ 86339-1783

ISBN 0-9688648-0-5

For Elizabeth, Toby and TS

CONTENTS

Parents

Growing up I found it almost impossible to figure out what my parents wanted out of life. As far as I could tell they were nice people. They never cheated on one another that I knew of or betrayed a friend or committed crimes that have prison terms attached to them. They had deep feelings about things, I'm sure, but I grew up in the 1950s, a time when strong emotions were out of fashion. I think they loved each other. They regularly told each other they did. All forty-one years of their marriage they slept together in the same narrow maple spool bed which had originally been given to his parents as a wedding present.

What you've just read is, of course, a load of crap. I lived with these people for 18 years. Nice people? Are you kidding? Living with them was heaven and hell all at the same time — a painful, joyous, confusing, humiliating, uplifting, frustrating experience. It was my life, the whole of it. We were part of each other, flesh and blood, bound together in the belly of the beast. There was nothing any of us could do about it.

At different times I thought they were bums, losers, compromisers, fearful and ignorant screw-ups and they thought the same about me. At others they were the finest of human beings, pictures of true understanding, the best parents a boy could ever hope for. We loved, hated and ignored each other with as much emotion as our tender hearts would allow.

We argued, laughed, fought and ate thousands and thousands of meals together. Year in, year out we carried on a babbling, zig-zag conversation full of passion, common sense, profound insights, plain lies and inconsequential bullshit. My blessed parents drove me nuts, they took me to the edge of true joy and contentment. I was a huge disappointment to them and I was their greatest joy. We hurt each other terribly, betrayed each other in ways nobody else could. There was nothing we wouldn't do for one another. And none of it ended even after they were in their graves. I talk to them still. Welcome to family life.

My mother was an intellectual who teased my sister and me by speaking Middle English while washing the dishes. She was the fastest and worst cook I ever knew; even so, I always looked forward to sitting down at her table. She taught retarded kids at school who loved her to such lengths they'd follow her home and stand outside the house for hours hoping for a glimpse of her. Her friends thought she was the happiest most generous person they'd ever hoped to meet. Alone in the house she could give Job a run for his money, beseeching God to give her grace and patience. There were times I knew beyond question in my heart of hearts she was the shallowest, most self-centered person on earth, one with the sensitivity of an echidna, and that that was doing a disservice to the echidna.

My father was a Vermonter, taciturn and patrician, about as intellectual as a sugar maple when the sap's running. His family had owned a saw mill and half a town on the Canadian border. By the time I came along the trees were long gone and so was the money. All that remained were a set of old yankee values — part-Christian, part miser and 100% horse-sense — and some fine porcelain dishes and engraved silver, most of it wrapped in 1930s' newspapers and stored in three big wooden barrels in the basement. He knew how to behave and God forsake the son who stepped over the line. Transgressions were left to rot in the long grass like a crop of neglected apples, never mentioned, never forgotten.

He could spot a fine antique or a well-cut suit at thirty paces. He never had more than a thousand dollars in the bank and never acted as though he had less than half a million. He could drink beer with the boys at the plant and make polite conversation with a countess. He was famously charming with old ladies and they adored him for it. Mostly, though, he was a silent man who kept his demons to himself. The few times I got a glimpse of what might be going on inside, I'd wished I hadn't. He had a volcanic temper. The prodigious and terrifying magna of those eruptions was composed mostly of ancient swear words and the banging of fists. You didn't want to be in the vicinity when the top blew.

What provoked these explosions and when they would occur was as unpredictable as earthquakes along the San Andreas fault. At fifty he was the spitting image of Henry Miller and my literary friends used to beg for invitations to the house just so they could sit in the same room with him. I doubt if he ever read Miller or any of the other masters of twentieth century prose. Truth be told, I never saw him read a novel. His taste in poetry ran to Longfellow and Robert Service and he delighted in spewing out long passages from *Hiawatha* or *The Shooting of Dan McGrue* while taking a bath or stirring up a pot of butter-heavy oyster stew. He was a wonderful scratch cook and not a man to shower.

Mother may have headed her class in honors English at college but the only works on our shelves were mysteries and a large collection of *Reader's Digest* Condensed books. I don't think either one of them ever attended a ballet, a symphony or an opera and the only theater that could get them out of the house was a comedy or a whodunit that had had a long run and good reviews.

For all its heft and feel, my growing years took place in the blandest decade in the century and the times took their toll on the family. For months on end we acted for all the world like good little Protestants following the good little Protestant work ethic. I remember interminable periods that were so utterly dull and predictable, so without joy or terror, I was ready to slit my throat. For all that, twisted and conflicting currents beneath the surface constantly buffeted my parent's relationship and my sister and I paid the price, even if we weren't always aware of it.

We both left home as soon as we were able to support ourselves, she to paint and I to begin my struggles as a writer. Robert Frost might well have composed our protest anthem in his poem about a spring swollen creek titled *One step backward taken*. It goes, in part, like this:
"Not only sands and gravels,
Were once more on their travels,
But gulping mighty gallons,
Great boulders off their balance,
Bumped heads together dully,
And started down the gully,

Whole cakes caked off in slices,
I felt my standpoint shaken
in the universal crisis,
But with one step backward taken,
I saved myself from going,
A world torn loose went by me,
Then the rain stopped and the blowing,
And the sun came out to dry me."

My father loved hotels

My father loved hotels and smoking cigarettes,
On an oppressive August day when I was ten,
He wheeled the '47 oil-guzzling Oldsmobile
up to the Bretton Woods Hotel in New Hampshire,
where Roosevelt and Churchill met during the war.
He got out in his baggy seersucker pants,
a white nylon dress shirt sweat-pasted to his back,
slammed the door hard and lit a Pall Mall.
We drove off moments later in a shabby blue halo of exhaust,
My sister and I trembled in the big gray-clothed back seat
and stared out our separate sides at the endless trees,
He had to stop twice to add oil from a case he kept in the trunk,
Outside Bellingham, Mass., he said in a soft voice,
"Seventy-two bucks."
We spent the night at the $11 Lone Pine Cabins,
He was the kindest man I knew.

Ten years later I worked for an airline slinging baggage,
The pay was good and I could get family tickets
and hotel passes for almost nothing.
I had married badly and he knew it,
He and my mother flew to Miami and New Orleans,
They stayed at the Fontainebleau and at Beaume's,
he ate Oysters Rockefeller and drank rye,
They stayed two nights at the St. Francis in San Francisco,
For years he wouldn't talk about the trip,
It was too good to spoil.

He had trouble with his feelings
And a bad temper I inherited.
He could scare even his favorite grandchildren

"Eat your damn potatoes," he'd burst at the supper table
and bring his fist down hard.
On Sundays in the early '50s,
He'd tuck a wintergreen Lifesaver between his gum
and his upper lip
And we'd all troop off to the forgiving
Finchly Street United Church,
I never understood what he believed in,
He was an usher for thirty-one years,
Old ladies would line up at the back of the church
For the privilege of taking his arm,
He slept during the sermon,
Walking home he'd produce the half dissolved Lifesaver
And laugh.

My father died

My father died without saying anything,
As though his words of comfort
with my name in them,
Caught in his throat like a fish bone
And killed him.

I went from loneliness to loneliness,
The way I suppose now he had,
Forever on the verge
Of some unsayable sweetness.

Don't forget me, please, don't forget me

My pastel mother
Disappearing
As though so many moths
were eating holes in her mind.
There is no way of telling
what it is she can't remember.
After a conversation
as normal as an autumn apple
She asks how my job is going at *Reader's Digest*,
where I have never worked.
What good does it do to deny that
of which others are so certain?
We are all keepers of our own truths.
I tell her I am happy and busy as usual
editing "Humor in Uniform"
And she sails on
Serene
Into unknown territory.

I didn't love my mother always

My mother is dead.

Her face turned ghastly
And the soul went out of her
like a puff of wind,
Leaving only what was bad in her
for us to bury.

Two years pass.

Some days I can feel
The earth working her way around the sun
in my innards.
I didn't love my mother always,
But I want her to love me,
To feel the long silvery arms of who she is
Reach out and draw me into silence.

The desires of the dead

My sister asked
Gravel & Son
To carve our mother's name
Underneath our father's
On the family stone.

"Lying here you see clouds
And fir trees,
A northern sky random as thought,
Exquisite dawns.
Icy days when nobody's around
Are some of the best.
Astonishing sunsets,
And the grass in June,
Marvelous!
Soft yellow shoots, then green and sharp
Then brown
And the snow,
Such a comfort,
Soft, deep, silent,
Something you can take forever
To know.
God hides in the world
Mindless as faith.

Look, here comes a man with a lawn mower,
And a chisel.
How sweet."

*L*ove

I took love for granted until I was into my teens. Then, for a long time, love meant sexual love. Lying naked with a girl was all the love and why. I have loved dogs and children. I've loved my parents and my friends and loathed them at the same time. Flowers, forests, lakes, rivers, rocks, oceans, islands, mountains, especially trees, have my love and have never abused it. The night sky enchants me, I have often fallen under the spell of the moon. I have learned to love silence and solitude and have looked there for love. What I found was not love but light and that has made some small difference.

The poems that follow are about romantic love and those other kinds of love.

Good morning

You open your eyes and sound
fills all the spaces in the room,
As though everything you are
has become symphony.
Between the plain beige sofa
And the floaty curtains,
Your whole landscape rings,
Vast forests appear, deep as history,
Long fields furrowed with new corn,
wheat, millet,
Buttercups, daisies, Queen Anne lace among the chorus of
long winnowing grass,
Beside your singing rivers.
Far towns and hidden gardens spun with
Lupines, foxglove, saffron poppies,
Echo the silken secrets of your heart,
Wind flutes the high sky, climbed with clouds
And shapes worlds in the ear that I
Have never glimpsed.

Blame it on peonies

I walk in the dark throat of the old city
Where peonies bloom behind windy walls,
Women pass in light dresses
Like lives untired.

Hurricane season

The wind you wore so lightly,
the one in the eyes of the animals who trusted us,
Curls under the ivy
As we curl in bed,
Takes down the summer green
That had protected us for so long
from the city, the mountains beyond the river,
the midnight rain, the others.
Fear framed itself over the flooded fireplace
Took down our disguises –
Though they were cold and false
We embraced them like fame and money.
When it is over,
We take the dogs for a walk in Summit Park,
The trees put on their seasons, take them off,
Is it really time again to put away another summer?
Autumn already hangs in the closet,
Winter is folded in the trunk at the foot of the bed,
Spring sings her soft mad songs behind the furnace,
A rose sleeps in the palm of your hand,
I sleep in the light it encloses.

With you in Italy

I'll never touch your body with its scent of lemon,
Though it sings to me
So many nights,
As though I lay sleeping
In an orchard in Italy.

I dream more lives than there are blossoms,
And awake to find myself
Covered with touches and snow.

But a train won't bring you home...

On the timetable of the train you took that still day,
Is a photograph of the train you took,
That still day you moved imperceptively away,
Into the photograph of the train you took.

Half-cocked and lily-bold

Half-cocked and lily-bold
We slipped forgetful-thin
Through lilac-downpours
Where no water ran.

We danced
Light-shine light and laughed
Fickle as wind-flacked daisies
Whiffing on their hillsides
Not yet steep or level as a touch.

The springtime
Crystal-blown and kisses wide
Was all there is and why,
Or autumn still and always in the sky
Shook out the day
With secrets made of sighs,
Sang like a heart-still, mixed
What we did not know with why
And gently went to bed.

Full as love is round
We stirred and almost heard
The moon-rise swell
In orchards bent with golden pears
But slept past never-cares
And nearly knew
The snow does not leave traces when it goes.

How love lasts and does not

Downstairs in the porcelain museum,
The Chinese have moved into eternity.
Their intrigues arrested,
Their politics suspended,
They seem happier now.
Beside the lapis pool,
A soldier rests between orders,
The emperor discourses with his minister,
A lovely woman waits
In that rich moment before her lover's kiss.

Upstairs in the dining room,
We gather over lunch,
Colleagues, associates, competitors,
Cautious smiles, veiled conversations, heavy food,
Your face, pale as chrysanthemum petals,
Floats on the violet dusky air,
I want to tell you I love you,
The instant passes
And is gone.

What roses do

Remember the night
the moon wept on your shoulder,
in another rose time,
before we knew what roses do?
And that Elizabethan gentleman
Who offered you a rose so sweet
It seemed to come from an unseen world.

Is this what roses are?
Phantoms of our finer selves
That slip through into this world,
When we need them most,
The way love can,
Not only in moonlight?

Then it is done

She appears afterward like a flower distracted,
And he a branch of blossom in uncertain weather.
They understand well enough what earth is for,
Beyond that,
The terrible progression of spring –
And the other business –
Reputation, ambition, money, children –
Shadows on water,
Clouds over deserts,
The kind of love
That leaves no traces when it goes.

What we try to do for love

By the beach at Kitsilano
I gaze out on the gray-green water,
A regatta of sail and wind
flies down the far shore.
In the mouth of the bay
Heavy freighters wait like a trade war
To storm the beach.
A gay man goes by in flip flops,
A girl in a chartreuse bikini
lights her friend's cigarette,
A woman smacks her kid.

I am here for your wedding,
A pale man from the east,
Slightly jet-lagged, a little irritable,
Ill-prepared, as usual, for any seminal event.
Your father, remembering you at four on another beach,
In Spain, wearing a heavy, black, hand-knitted sweater
against the Easter wind,
How many nights I have been grateful
For those months together when you were so young
And I was crazy to make another life for myself.
I succeeded – though it took me twenty years to do it,
And you grew up despite me,
And were often better at caring than I was,
And now you are on the edge of marriage
To a woman I believe and hope everything for.

A small wind tosses a few twigs far out on the water
A sea-tide pulls away from the land,
What's left is love.

A garden is no substitute for love

White blooms float on midnight's limpid pool
Where the moon swims naked with desire,
A century of hollyhocks haunt the sky,
Cosmos, their hillside blood, invades our dreams
like bits of half forgotten songs:
The stranger's touch that binds the breath,
The lover's hurtful wrongs.

What secrets do nasturtiums take a summertime in learning
If not that they and earth are one in undivided yearning.

Come, sit with me on cupid's bench
It is time for the naming of flowers.
These roses make no promises,
A garden is no substitute for love,
And beauty keeps her council to the end.

The heart's trembling architecture

What constitutes the heart's trembling architecture?
Is it aloneness? Silence?
Light that pours from the inside of things?
That certain face, a look, ordinary days?
Songs of blessing and of praise?
The sky in a mirror?
A window overlooking a river?
The unmade bed?
An unfamiliar touch, the shiver
That comes from knowing and unknowing?
What we give up when love has shed its secrets?
The compounded beauty of a flower?
An old and empty tower?
Starlight falling on a field?
Long grasses above the heart's sheer drop
Into the unspeakable wonder of the sea?

Mayan cities we visit now and then

Let the mind rest lightly
On these praising stones
Untroubled by the earth of blood and bones.
The sun shines still,
Blue bubbles rise in cisterns
And they always will.
The moon casts her silver shadow
like a fisher's net
To capture Mars and Venus
When the sun has set.

Let my mind rest lightly on your face
What can it matter where our fingers trace
Or do not trace?
Or what we say or what we're thinking of?
When all these things we love are gone
There'll still be love.

People

A tree surgeon once told me, "I care about what people think of me," and added, "It's a sad thing." He was a difficult man, a drunk and not a pleasant one. He smelled bad and had regrets. When he said it, tears gathered in my eyes and I turned away so he wouldn't notice.

The characters in the poems that follow include friends, enemies, strangers — even a fish. How they got into my heart and into these poems is a mystery. They include a man trying to sell his house, a woman in love watching a movie about a woman in love with someone who doesn't love her, a monk and a killer, a private eye, Marilyn Monroe, JFK and a man with heart as big as Africa. Like the healer of trees, I care what they think of me. It's a sad thing.

There are people with hummingbirds in them

In Granada — and elsewhere —
There are people with hummingbirds in them,
Delicate and iridescent,
Nearly invisible as souls.
Lorca could see them
Bless the fruited summer air,
Hover in a honied eye,
Stand still above the heart.
Once you've seen something like that,
You don't have to believe in God anymore,
Everything you need's inside you.

What happens to hands when they become famous?

For JFK and MM

What is it about artichokes? Mystery?
Layer after layer. Ever more tender. Vulnerable.
And at the center? Secrets.
What is it about small hands?
Dolly has hands as small as flowers,
Where she places them rain falls.
He says, "Your hands remind me of roses."
She says, "Make it gardenias and I'm yours.
I want to be wonderful."
He thinks of Jesus. Those surrendered hands
that washed pale feet.
When he looks up, she has long ago
been crowned Artichoke Queen.
And their love has become so famous
They can no longer touch it.

Taking tea with Mrs. Ming

The vase tipped by a golden bug
Goes mingling with the Persian rug,
The walls become another chair
Inside the roses over there,
The marble table blows and drifts
Among the flowers and the cliffs
Drape bushes as the thickets ride
Over to the other side
Where molecules of afternoon,
The teacup and the silver spoon,
Play their lemon colored tricks,
Blending milk cows in the mix
Of what you are and what was me
And other liquid symphonies.
When sun and moon are on the lam,
Love comes to lion and to lamb,
Then silence is the sound we hear,
Heart music in the inner ear.

What was empty is filled again

Taos February morning, Sunday,
Blue smoke weaves straight into ice colored air,
A man with a good face,
And a badge pinned to his western flannel shirt,
Nods and kicks at the snow with his boot.
Inside the Casino,
Two men watch tv
Behind a row of vacant slots.
Smoky sunlight spills in through big windows,
Igniting Saturday night's experienced air.
There are no players.

The famous pueblo, dawn-mottled, orange-brown,
Five jagged stories high,
Skin of an angular beast cut with rough ladders,
Sighs against the indigo of the sacred mountain,
A woman carries a large jar across the plaza,
Two dogs follow her.
One stops and looks back.

A heart as big as Africa

Suppose a man worked in an office
And had a heart as big as Africa,
At his desk, he shakes his head
As if the morning lay bleeding,
He wants to take off his shoes,
escape into shadow.
He sees, in the middle distance,
Storm clouds with faces in them gather up the world,
all green and violet,
An evil wind groans in the thorn tree.
It is as though he is dead and is
looking back on his life,
A part of who he was will not let go of him.

He stands up,
Paces back and forth in the narrow hall,
The eyes of his heart look downward,
Through dust-startled air, to the earth,
the fire,
These things listen, but when he reaches out
they turn away and mock him.

Other days he has no strength,
He blames it on powerful animals
who have no names,
He calls them his keepers.

Those things we have in common with salmon

She says: "Try the pear and roses pie,"
"And would you love me then?"

A dog barks at his own echo out of a windy moon,
What is the universe we see in the night sky?
A progression of numbers not different from a sheaf of tears,
And not what it ever seems to be,
And what defines the light
That falls through the dirty window of this far off café?

"Try the pear and roses pie, you'll like it
And I'll love you then."

On another page,
The English mathematician's daughter
Dreams she sleeps with a salmon,
As he climbs the staircase of rapids, his silver tail
Slaps her broad backside over and over,
She moans, the salmon wonders: "Is this the moment?"
He longs for better breeding, a better death,
A different system of numbers.
Why should we be kind?

Poem noir

Who doesn't have something they're looking for? He says to her
— Baby, wise up. It's yourself.
Parts of town you can't walk in anymore. And don't talk to me
about the mayor.
Here's a civics lesson for ya. They chopped down all the oaks in
England in the sixteen hundreds. I'm no dumbie. Alexander
Sprogget with his little axe took down 30,000, all by his lonesome.
Chop, chop, chopping until he kicked at 80. The great
Northwest. Just like déjà-vu all over again.
Know what I'm saying?
Tell ya this, I'm glad the martini is back. And the way the sky
spreads out over the city still all violet in the evening. Pretty.
And so many evenings.
So ya read palms, sister? Read this!
I'm going to have a medium-length life. Ha. Ha. Ha. I drink too
much. Am not careful. Butts. No exercise. Heavy. Romance?
Lots but not the right kind.
In the car, she wept.
So what if I'm into fedoras and marble railroad stations. You got
a problem with that, pal? I read somewhere doublet and hose are
making a comeback. And not just the queers wearing them
either. Better take a Pasadena on that one. But, like it says in
the Good Book, help yourself.
This broken man goes into an empty church, see. Asks Jesus,
Mary, God Almighty about this and that. Gets some answers, not
others. Am I right or am I right?
Ya got lovely legs, I'm saying to myself. And a Modigliani face.
Which ain't great but it ain't bad either. Flesh tones. Hard
angles. Of course, I want to see you naked.
It's like this, I'd do anything you ask, almost. Whadda ya say?
Thinking about your situation. It has to do with the relationship
with your, ah, father. And never getting what you want from, ah,
men. Your mother? Who would say anything against your mother?

Money? Don't think of it. It's been taken care of. Drive down to the corner of Hollywood and Vine at one AM. Observe the stars from the back seat of a convertible.

When there's water in the east, the wise prosper. Gimme a hug and a smack for the road. I'm outta here.

How to live in the physical world

Here's the thing: To arrange your life like geometry,
Foreign travel has something to do with it. Stars.
Watching Orion pass from left to right from a deck chair,
Rooms should be done in pink or not at all,
And make them faded, mottled, as though the walls were part of
the living that's gone on there. Same goes for yellow. Blue? A disaster.
Animals help set a certain tone, not without a price. Who hasn't
envied them their fur?
"Put the house over there in the Belly of the Dragon," she said.
She has that presence, no one dares cross her. They call it wisdom.
You have interests in vineyards, your hands betray you. And in
things Dutch. Stalin thought Holland and The Netherlands were
different countries.
It would not be intelligent to think all mass murderers were poorly
informed.
Perhaps it is easier to see things as they really are. We get such ideas!
Let's all hold hands and come out against clutter once and for all.
I have to tell you, I admire your wife, even under that silly hat.
Tell her when I've gone. Use words like "orange" or "lavender."
Say: "When I look at you I see castles (angels, fields of wild
flowers, poppies, dancers) behind you." It's been used before but
so little is truly original, would you agree?
Something, perhaps, to do with water, night skies, the claims so
many even good people have made on the moon,
Promises. Water, yes, water.
Do let's dress up as Alice Springs on the hypotenuse,
There's a knighthood coming in. Can't you feel it?

Cabaret Shakespeare

The brown Missisquoi flows golden to the lake, stitched to the
meadow by blue dragonflies, this Sunday in July.
How many times has the car hesitated, almost pulled in
to the Blue Ford Café?
Is there a poem hidden in there someplace, taped under a table
like a knife under plate of picnic chocolate cake?
Does Old John the Vagabond sit by a window slurping coffee
out of his saucer anxious for conversation after all these years?
In Spain decades ago, he was so good at caging drinks.
You remember him, don't you? His best line by far was: Where
to go and what to write about?
Esteban, mas mantilla, another glass for my friend,
You were reading King Lear,
I was already a father,
The other day the phone line from Moscow was terrible,
Something about a night club in Luxembourg, a dancer,
The most beautiful girl in the world.
Was that what you said?
You have a new son, Max?
Your life was turning into literature?
There was so much static you might have said almost anything,
Garbage in the streets, for example, or how they'd turned the hot
water off in May,
We've tried to make a life, God knows, waited as patiently as
the others,
A change in the weather? A morning with a new feel about it?
Garçon, deux formidable, vite, a flagon of words, a new world
order, a nice piece of ass,
Who wants to be famous? Fulfillment, there's the ticket,
Have I told you about my meditations?
17 years of silence. You can get as good at this stuff as death if

you put your heart into it.
Funny thing is, it's made me more interested in the world and
less in the here after,
I look at cows now quite differently,
take pleasure in smaller and smaller things,
I'm not boasting, I'm shrinking.
Have you stopped smoking like everyone else? I'd be surprised.
Up here in Vermont sometimes I could give up memory entirely,
My wife has a passion for Russian dogs,
We have a pet pig, Victoria, age 8,
Who doesn't make it up as they go along?

Remake of La Strada

Small angels fluttered from your hands like colored silks
As though you were a magician on the cusp of the unseen.
You spoke from somewhere you had already gone beyond,
And that had left you open to the suffering of others.
What had been the world was the world no longer,
You sighed over the dog on the bicycle, so dear, so hungry,
The tears of the clown, the strong man —
his ambition and his anger,
And especially for those who love without hope.
You wanted so badly for things to be right again.
I had to turn away:
You were crying for those who want to change their lives.

I come from Barcelona

Where I come from is Barcelona,
That crooked city, that splendor,
The churches with their gaudy crucifies,
That twist their way into your heart,
I am the legless man you passed in Las Ramblas,
The crimson night when you were high
on love and riojas,
I am the mendicant,
The one who gives and receives,
The happy fool.

On the seafront at sunset,
I walk with the man in the white suit,
His violet-eyed wife holds our secret tenderly,
like a new born,
The wonder of her body,
Its hungers,
The way, when midday glitters at the shutters,
Her hair spells my name in shadows,
Across the starched white pillow case,
On the boundary of love and death.

I left on the narrow gage train
that climbs into the mountains,
It was in February, that damp, useless month,
The revolver in my knapsack,
The wooden box of cartridges,
My passport presumed I was a citizen of France.
Paris was as luminous as a green apple that spring,
There were tiny lilies in the Luxembourg,
You twisted them in your hair.

When the moment came, I couldn't do it.
It didn't trouble me, the idea that I was a coward,
Now that we are here, safe, in a country
neither of us chose,
The atrocious weather, the damaged economy,
I've lost track of who was the betrayer,
who the betrayed.
How do I spend my days?
That little church on the river,
The one with the gold Madonna and child,
I pray there at dawn,
It's a quiet life,
As suits an assassin,
I miss my wife and child, Larisa, these blue nights.
Before I put on these colored robes,
I felt that family life was everything,
I have learned to focus on God,
For the last hour I have thought of nothing,
As though I were some old Russian pilgrim,
Walking in winter on a road that runs through birches
Fixed only on inner weather.

Artists

A while ago, I was in Galerie D'Avignon in Montreal, an unpretentious spot run by Marian Read and her doctor husband Andreas Giannakis. It was a cold Sunday in late fall and business was anything but brisk. The lack of customers didn't seem to bother the good doctor a bit. He talked about the pleasures of running an art gallery. "It's being able to get to know the artist's that I like most," he said. "They're not like the rest of us. They see life in a different way."

We chatted for an hour or so about some of the painters we both knew. They were, of course, a motley bunch. Some drank too much, smoked too much marijuana or sniffed, ingested or injected copious amounts of other substances. Others piled up debts or were horribly insensitive to the needs of anyone close to them, especially their spouses and children. Some talked incessantly and others didn't utter a word for days on end. Still others were the kindest, gentlest souls you could hope to meet. They had little in common, we agreed, except for one thing; each had a unique way of viewing the world and life around them.

Here are some of the writers and poets whose visions of what it is to be human strike a chord in me.

RAINER MARIA RILKE. For his ability to evoke the powerful forces behind the veil that form and reform physical life. For his determination to live life as a poet. And for his glorious name.

FREDERICO GARCIA LORCA. There are many reasons to love his work but I have only three simple ones: for his earth and trees and flowers. And, perhaps, a fourth: for his Spanish countryside. I visited the house where he grew up just outside Granada on the 30th anniversary of his assassination. A hot afternoon in summer. A newly planted orchard. No one around. Except for the buzzing of insects, silence.

LEONARD COHEN. Cohen grew up in Montreal and was recognized as a wonderful poet in his teens. *Spice Box of Earth,* his second book was, for a long time, my favorite book of poems.

Woody Allen jokes about how fans seem to prefer his "early films." I might say the same about Cohen except that I have copies of all his albums, know most of the words by heart and read both his novels — *The Favourite Game* and *Beautiful Losers* — in hardcover as soon as I could get my hands on them. It doesn't hurt that he loves Lorca.

BOB DYLAN. For his rhymes, his subjects, the vast range of his interests, his endless life on the road and, yes, for his voice.

RUMI. For me – and I'm scarcely alone – his work is a fountain fed by the Ocean of Ilm (divine luminous wisdom). Of the tens of thousands of lines that flowed from that fountain, consider only five: "Tear the binding from around the foot / of your soul, and let it race around the track / in front of the crowd. Loosen the knot of greed / so tight around your neck. Accept your new good luck."

SRI CHINMOY. For his endless songs of the heart which pour like a vast river not only from *his* soul, but from the soul of the world. Not yet widely known, he has written perhaps a hundred thousand poems and aphorisms.

WALLACE STEVENS. For his job as vice-president of the Hartford Accident and Indemnity Company. For his love of solitude: "I detest company and do not fear any protest of selfishness in saying so." And for his poems, not one of which I have ever fully understood but which I have been unable to stop reading.

ROBERT FROST. For New England.

TOM WAITS. For his drinking piano. For his gigantic sentimentality for the real. And, yes, for his voice.

VIRGINIA WOOLF. For her understanding of how we are all always children. For her first chapters in *The Waves*. For *To the Lighthouse*. For her suffering.

EMILY DICKINSON. For the way she could make common words dance to a new tune.

There are many more, of course. Sylvia Plath, Anne Sexton, Adrienne Rich, John Ashbury, Shelly, Keats, Yeats, Blake, John Clare and dozens and dozens of other poets whose work I've read and cherished for years or for an afternoon. To all those both remembered and forgotten, my soul's deepest gratitude.

Henry Miller vanishes in the light

This started as a story.
Henry would have understood that—
who has the patience for poetry these days?
It's about how, when he died,
He went to China
And vanished in the light,
Just like he said he would.
It's a story about the wonder of the world,
About *homo sapiens*, you and me,
And not about how we get screwed up either,
It's about how we become glorious,
Like Henry Miller did.

Here's our hero now,
Coming down the gangplank
Of the Star Ferry from Kowloon.
Notice his fedora
Pushed back on the glistening dome of his pate,
His sparkling eyes,
The smoothness of his skin,
His happy gait,
Like someone who has seen through to the other side.
He's humming to himself, a happy song,
Like the ones he sang in Paris in the '30s
After a good meal and a glass or two of red,
After a squirmy dance in a smokey club,
After paying for a lovely piece of tail
And taking his pecker for a walk
Along the Seine in the rain,
Or after being kind and radiant in Brooklyn
Or out on the west coast,
That song being the one
In which the joke's on him,

And how he wanted to be kind and generous,
And how sometimes he was and sometimes he wasn't,
How the universe keeps things in balance,
As how at 87 he falls head over heels
For some Japanese café singer-hooker,
Whom he marries
And who takes him for
Everything he's got,
That little ditty he whistles
As he climbs the steep hills of Hong Kong,
Called "No fool like an old fool."
The merry dance, the dismal jig,
And how he realized near the end of it
It didn't matter a flying fuck,
"I chose sex, Jake,
What did you choose?"
He thought for a while
He'd become a Buddha.
On his hill in Big Sur,
Already old, forsaken,
How in shit did he know
He'd live another 30 years,
Up there in a shack over the Pacific,
Painting watercolours to keep the wolf away,
Cursing his publishers,
Poor as spit,
Celebrated as sand,
And not a nice man either.
The wife, the kids,
Give us this day our daily grind,
Let thy will be done,
And all the while his crazy cock
Becoming so famous
It practically ruined everything.
"I chose sex, Jake,
What did you choose?"
And the writing finally became
Only something to do.
Like mending clothes or planting fields.

And here he comes now
To a makeshift temple
Thrown up on a busy slope,
Crowded in by cheap shops
Selling gaudy plastic do-dads.
The sun shines,
The air smells of Chinese cooking,
Incense and dog crap.
He hums to himself,
"I was a bad man, I was a good man,"
And he thinks about
Faces, eyes, mouths, kisses,
Hands, feet, flowers, bike rides.
He kneels down on his crumbly knees,
And puts his papery lips
To Buddha's gold and plaster feet,
A band plays,
Children laugh and sing,
Henry Miller vanishes in the light.

Death as an electric train

For Catherine Widgery on her one-woman show

It is as though children from another world
Have fallen out of the sky,
Their beauty impaled on trees and towers,
Broken against the earth, its flatness,
Yet they retain their joy.

Where did they come from?
How did they keep their extraordinary gifts?
Their playfulness?
Could there also be something inside of us
That remembers death is a doorway into lightness?

How can you tell the poet from the poems?

O that Percy Bysche, speed demon,
Wrecked his racing sloop
In ten foot waves on Lake Geneva,
Too much sail,
Too much wind,
Too many women,
Bad debts,
Bad politics,
He went down screaming,
"No, No," against the wind-shear,
Another terrible mistake.

The water stopped what he could not stop,
That ferocious energy,
Fanny's suicide, Harriet's,
His babies dying in Italy.

They brought his body back
And Byron burned it on the shore,
His poems rising like rockets into eternity
On the fiery after-burners
Of his short, fierce life.

Born in Vermont

The winter afternoon burns slowly down,
In a white house in Vermont I read Paul Blackburn,
Hard-luck poet, born in St Albans, 1926,
Not far from here.
A railway town, now tough and idle,
I learned to swim in the lake there, 1953,
The writer died in New York City, 1971,
Of throat cancer and
Mostly, so many lines seem to say, of
The losing struggle to get it down right,
Years piled on the years of watching
Love under the broken sky,
Recording, refining, getting better
Nearing the point beyond which
Nothing and everything matters.
Chesterfields and February.

Yet, again, the lover,
Cara mia, my one, my only,
Light of my life,
Boards a train in some provincial town,
The tearing sleet comes down,
She will not be back.

He walks along the seawall,
In Spain, 1957,
The salt water glistens like a sleeper,
The broken scribbling of waves, of dreams,
Of worse, of words,
A dirty little wind kicks at the sand,
A woman in black hunched over

By a loss similar to his
Passes him and spits.

The poet looks out on the tools of his craft,
This sea of rough material
Of which he hopes to make something
Worthy of eternity.

In the frozen clouds he sees St Albans,
And hears again an icy freight shuttle in the yard,
The cold clank of steel on steel,
Blue smoke rises straight up.
The sky presses on the land like a glacier,
Winter has her way with him.

Portrait of the artist as a young girl

For Susan Elkins

Young mountains embrace you
and your dress of ribbons and wind,
High places braid themselves in your hair,
come out in your paintings,
What is the world except a way of seeing?

Your love of light has made you its enduring friend,
you who taught yourself how to look,
Light plays with you, holds you in the night,
Stars press themselves to your skylight.
Their aloneness
Binds you to them,
As though you too
have traveled from a distant world.

Earth, its kindness, rushes to meet you,
Remakes itself in your trees and empty houses,
Places where good people struggled,
Color spawns in your eyes,
Helps us, we for whom the sky means almost nothing,
To see.

And everything is one

Vincent wrote to his brother Theo,
"Christ was a great man
because he had no furniture,"
And the universe tilted,
The sky cart-wheeling,
Suns falling into gardens,
What he saw he knew
Others could not see.

In his narrow hired bed
He lay very still
Listening to his reputation
Grow among the irises,
He could see the future.
Fear blossomed on the side of his head,
The room swirled,
And he became again,
A point of light,
No different from all the others
He tried dizzy to capture.

Visitors

For Richard Roblin

Color rushes in a field of fire,
A far sun in love with a tattered ocean,
Gold, orange, blue, white, midnight,
Things we loved and had forgotten,
Things we've seen,
And done and not done,
The way we came.

Who could have expected a life like this one?

A woman who has been crying steps into an elevator,
Someone you wish you could love again smiles in a mirror,
The tracings of clouds, a door in the sky,
Silence, a ringing in the ears,
A troubled monk wades in a stream,
What heart has not contained the tranquility of sand,
The slow beauty of moss?
A woman bends to a child,
A man moves a hand to his forehead aware his life has shifted,
Saturn stands above the crescent moon, a thumb width to the north,
The lines of our lives blur,
Release us.

Breakfast with García Lorca

García Lorca came to breakfast in his white suit,
He offered to play the lute,
His hands, I remember, were cold,
As though he were wearing gloves made of water,
When they heard the first chords,
The cups and saucers clapped their hands and cheered:
"Play on Maestro, we'll wait for coffee."
The table sang along in Spanish, a language I didn't know it knew,
While a yellow bowl of blue gentians stamped out the rhythm,
Oh and the room filled up with bees, so happy to be invited
They'd forgotten their stings.
When the music stopped,
The chairs fought over which one he would sit in,
And the rug threatened to roll up
If it could not be under his feet,

His eyes explained the catachism of sacrifice
As he peeled an apple and then a pear,
He amused them in their final moments with a story
He'd picked up from an orange grove in Valencia,
His face changed and became clouds over mountains,
By the time I felt the sea tugging at my sleeve
He had already gone.

What earth does not forget

The house spins in an unfamiliar garden,
A thousand mirrors reflect the waltzers of another era,
Their gowns of tears, the gentlemen dressed as thunder,
Snow poppies press against the window panes
For a glimpse of what they remember too well,
(His soul lingers in an upstairs bedroom, disguised as a desk.)
Zephyrs keep time in the apricots,
They too wish to forget
The blood which the pomegranate cannot,
In her grief, contain.

Gun shots!
Bullets rush forward screaming to cover their cowardice,
The spot where he falls cries out,
"Sing to me, sir,
Please, please sing to me.
Do not make me famous by dying here.
What bit of dust could wish for that?"

The pomegranate slams the door of her house,
And will not come out,
Even when the stars entreat her to
Night after night for sixty years,
She weeps and says,
"Things do not change."

A heart floating on the sea

We come out of the damp December air
Of Venice,
Cold, disoriented by the architecture,
The secret passageways, the sudden squares,
The narrow greenness of the salt canals
And a web of feeling
Intensified by our short time together,
Of being here, in this unlikely season.
Half the afternoon we wander
In fog and frozen mist,
Half lost,
Half restless yet content,
As though we had become,
Like the republic,
The protectors of dreams.

In an hour it will be dark.
We enter the gloomy gallery
The pictures tower over us like myths.
You whisper:
"God, this painting,
The Annunciation..."
A flock of angels flees into heaven,
Mary kneels radiant,
The Dove of Peace
Hovers in the icy air,

Under the scaffolding,
Tintoretto paces back and forth,
He mutters over the room's gloomy perspective
Why had he chosen this difficult space?

Why these massive scenes?
Arthritis burns his fingers.
In the day's last cold shadows
He goes down to San Marco
To pray for the strength to finish.

You turn to say something about yesterday,
What's done is done.
My heart floats on the surface of the sea.
The archangel Gabriel
Moves toward Mary like a lover.
She seems to draw back,
As any woman might.

Dogs

For the last thirty years, I've shared my life with dogs. There's little I won't do for dogs and, as far as I can tell, nothing they won't do for me. I mean this in the broadest sense. They won't sit, lie down, fetch sticks for me or even necessarily come back when called. They won't bring me my slippers or even promise to bark at strangers who might invade the house at midnight. I won't always take them for walks even when they're desperate to go, scratch them every time they roll over or even feed them on a reliable schedule. I'll even go away and leave them with strangers for a week or ten days. Still, together or apart, we never forget one another. We're always glad to see each other and are significantly happier and more evenly balanced when the other is around. We know what love is between us and never go against it.

The wolf who lives on the sofa

A wolf lives on the sofa in the front room.
Her name is her secret; she has yellow eyes,
Wherever her gaze falls she creates a vastness.
At night she takes everyone in the house,
Out running with the pack.
We can't resist her. We have tried.

Through the blurred evergreens
We catch glimpses of empty churches,
Starlit domes above rotting altars,
We need this space; this open country.
We pray for another kind of life.

When guests come at Christmas, they are afraid,
She lolls on her powerful back
And shows off her double row of teats,
Her sex glows like a forest flower.
They huddle together at the far end of the room,
And murmur in low voices.
Only after the meal,
Has been reduced to bone and gristle,
The best china licked clean,
Do we dare praise her gentle snores,
And count again on those stars she pointed to,
To guide our midnight meditations.

Bulldog Tao

There are whole days that I, Elizabeth,
Dream on the sofa,
My eyes gaze in at idleness, its exquisite pleasures,
I contemplate my powerful paws, my stuffed rabbit,
Come evening, someone brings my supper.
Before I sleep, I sniff the dark air, pee,
The moon, this universe of scents, familiar leaves,
Comfort me as I suppose they are supposed to do.

A bulldog's guide to small engine repair

One of those high mixed afternoons in late July,
The meadows a thousand-thousand flowers high,
Goldenrod, cornflower, milkweed, Queen Anne's lace,
And in the roiling air a trace
Of rain, the clouds piled up in towers,
Grand kingdoms for an hour,
The far wind rushes in the tops of trees
And scents the grass,
Thick and matted as young lovers' hair,
Where I work on a broken mower,
Metal mystery machine that's
Made a misery of two summers
Let the wild grass and mild neighbours mock.

I open the manual like the Book of Job,
Elizabeth, the bulldog foreman watches me,
Her bright and rheumy eyes
Lost in the wrinkles of her traveled face,
She's seen this all before, the pain
The curses to high heaven that leave me drained,
A confusion, a betrayal, and a curse,
The Book reads, lay the monster up on end,
Risking hernia and worse, I comply,
"Remove the catcher bar," it says,
"And then the undercarriage mens,"
"Release the camber springs. Remove
left and right guards." O what a treat!
"Replace the belt and in reverse — repeat."

The darkened underbelly of the thing reveals
No catcher bar, no guard, no camber spring,

What are the "mens?"
Just clumps of rust,
Only the ruined grass of yesteryear is here...
Those wretched years
Betrayed by kisses,
Promises not kept, the tears...
I lean a wrench against what might once have been a bolt,
It gives! And soon what might have been
A catcher bar is mine,
I scrape — and WD-40 in hand — I spray,
And tug, let go an oath and pray,
The under-carriage falls away,
The torn up days, the haze of raising stakes
When there were none to raise,
The springs come off — what's there?
Cylinder head, removed, cleaned out, replaced,
I swear, three shining pulleys spinning in the air,
I slip a new drive-belt on these Ezekiel's rings
That fire in the sky, what was I thinking?
Those blazes seen before, ignored,
Put out by drinking.
But I'm in a fresh new country now,
One made of steel, where things are sure,
And in a dream it's reassembled. Righted. Pure.
The engine grunts, coughs, catches, purrs,

What can be done except to gaze,
Upon this magic work — amazed,
The afternoon falls silent,
There's thunder in the far-off trees.
Elizabeth, fan, critic, friend, encourager.
Saunters over, licks my hand – and pees.

Alpha bitch

She arrived on earth
With nothing except
Knowing how to be a dog,
And huge enthusiasm,
And light,
Graceful as trees,
Without expectation
Except for immense happiness.

It wasn't easy,
The foster homes,
The jealousies,
Those who weren't always kind,
How could they be so blind
To her fine elegance?
She stood apart,
Took her own advice,
She exercised,
Ate well,
And didn't stint on loving
'Til love came back to her.

Lost dogs

Unleashed,
The dogs run off,
Disappear up the canyon,
Fleet, furry ghosts,
Fading into frost and dawn and junipers
Swift hunters after Jack rabbits
And who knows what?

A misty gown clings to the valley's beauty,
Hidden as the day,
I'm alone with possibility.

An hour goes
And I'm still alone, musing done, the day begun,
I'm ready to go home.
I find an echo and play with it for ten minutes,
The dogs' names keep coming back,
But not the dogs,
A small rain starts,
And blurs the view with cloud,
I'm deep in the canyon now
And need coffee.
The trail climbs a ridge
And drops into a secret meadow
Where dogs might hide, I seek,
I call and whistle, clap my hands,
Nothing.

They can move like shadows this pair of Russians hounds,
Brief as thoughts that give pleasure and are gone.
Full of grace.

They need exercise, I think,
They need freedom, I think,
Why won't the bastards come, I think.

Another hour gone and still no mutts,
Have they run clean to the next county?
Crossed the highway three miles off?
Been hit and killed?
Drowned in the creek?
Broken their slender legs in some bad fall?
Plunged into that sink hole near the tank?
Has some mad hunter gunned them down?
A pack of coyotes downed and eaten them?

Why is my life broken? Why can't I be kinder?
Finer? Get more done?
Why are there those who do not wish me well?
Others whom I cannot love?
The cliff hangs above the valley like a curse,
These damp trees were sent to make me mad.
Where are those damn dogs?

Hour four,
I've given up on finding them alive,
They're dead, hurt, bleeding,
What was their easy being for?
How he rolled his eyes and leaned into you
when told that he was good,
Her sideways smiles, her cobalt eyes,
the way she understood.
Now not open to the world
To flash like light against the hill
They can no longer move and never will.

I've walked eight miles,
Shouted my lungs out,
Nothing but silence and the rain's conspiracy.

Cruel clouds! You must have seen those borzoi,
Where have you buried them?

No breakfast, lunch, wet, angry, sad, undone,
When here she comes,
Subdued, covered with mud,
Her golden coat woven with burrs,
Smiling sideways as the circumstance requires:
"Here I am. A dog
Dogs do this."

Yes and where is he?
She trots back up the track,
Looking over her shoulder,
Follow me.
A quarter mile on he saunters
from a copse of trees,
And lies down in the path,
A tattered prince disgraced.

Prodigals!
Restored, alive, whole, perfect,
I breathe again,
Forgive even myself.

The rain comes on hard,
We're a long way from home,
And worthy of one another.

I have buried three dogs

For Aslan

I have buried three dogs
And already it is too many
For my heart.
But I will go on burying dogs
Until I too am buried,
For they are all joy
Until the unbearable sorrow
Of their running away,
Despite our desperate calls,
Into death.
And we must wait to follow.

Places

Was it the Sahara that first dreamed of pyramids? Did the Andes conceive of Machu Picchu; the high Himalayas first fantasize about Lhasa? Did Mount Fuji father the Japanese; England's Lake District appoint Wordsworth to be its singer of songs? Did Mecca breed Mohammed? Did the Black Forest lie down with the springs of the Rhine to birth a Goethe or a Hitler? Were Shakespeare's sonnets written by an Avon summer night?

Certainly places have had their way with me. I would not be who I am or think the way I do without Vermont. My moods and thoughts change when I'm in France or Greece or Spain or Canada. The emotions that tug at my heart in Taos, New Mexico, are strangers to the inner friends I meet in Seville or Manhattan or Montreal.

For a long time I fought against the power of place then, one starry night in the San Francisco mountains near Flagstaff, Arizona, I surrendered. The earth spoke to me through my feet. I stopped arguing and finding excuses. I just had to let it go. Tree, rock, hill, house, the way the land leans against the horizon now do with me what they will.

It's better this way.

Why trees love Joyce Kilmore

The thousand, thousand eyes of the trees turn downward,
They breathe in the dark the way we breathe,
The grasses are at their weaving,
Rocks at their incessant mumbling,
Sand and earth lie quietly, humble as always,
Knowing how much depends on them.
Together we absorb the moonlight.
After midnight,
The junipers take to boasting,
In a quiet way,
About how long they live —
And with so much grace and silence.

Bees and butterflies and peonies

Rosy-tipped and petal-parted,
Iron shields the day that's started,
The only heroes are the bees
and butterflies and peonies.
Grow grass, grow, up over the eaves.

River-bred and sandy-gotten
Silver dusts the fruit that's rotten,
The only theater is the bees
and butterflies and peonies.
Grow grass, grow up over the eaves.

Springtime-cursed and winter-branded
There is nothing underhanded
In breaking vows except to bees
and butterflies and peonies.
Grow grass grow, up over the eaves.

Seconds gnarl and hours harden,
Snow will close the brittle garden,
The enemies to slay are bees
and butterflies and peonies.
Grow grass grow up over the eaves.

Rural truths

*"The Ladies Aide of the Congregational Church will once more
be organizing their annual picnic and dance to be held, Saturday,
August 17, in Farmer Ladd's field adjacent to the cemetery. It is
hoped that this event will provide some relief to the local
populace from the monotony of country life."*
The Swanton Weekly Courier, August 1923

Again, again, again,
Wings afire, black birds,
Lift and dive,
Dive and lift again,
Rain rattles against the slanted light,
Of yet another afternoon,
Clouds form and reform,
Are lighted from within,
Turn chatreuse and mauve,
Pink and gold and orange,
Fields darken, an intimate wind swells in the west,
Predestined, the moon waxes, wanes,
Between the tedium of sunset and sunrise,
The same bright skein of stars,
Presides over the community of night,
Until the inevitable coo-cooing of doves.
A fresh wash of sky does nothing new,
Grackles congregate once more under the eaves,
Armless veterans of the weather wars,
Their minds ruined by the eternal cheerfulness of robins,
Beyond the fence, moonfaced cows
Ruminate on the infinity of grass
and their own gracious two stomached selves,
Puzzling for still another day

Whether to lie down or remain standing.
Alice and Willy, in their horsey prisons,
have rubbed against the same tree for twenty years,
Their conversation grown
Worn as the bark, clever as clover.
Perhaps the long-lived maples,
The fir, the poplar, the gossiping sumac,
Have some clue to the trickery of history,
But not even the wind's incessant curiosity
Can tease it out of them.
The pigs are numbed by endless mindgames,
The sheep are silly with sameness,
Even the hens are weary of the pecking order.
Master of the Universe, all creation cries to you,
In your infinite wisdom, we beg you, please
Deliver us from
The monotony of country life.

Downsides of cowdom

The rain came down so fiercely,
Over the sodden green pasture
I invited a Holstein in for tea.
Her name, she said, was Betsy,
And she was glad enough for the shelter
But she wouldn't have a hot drink,
Oh no, very bad for the stomachs, don't you know,
Cucumber sandwiches? I don't think so,
Gives you gas, I can tell you.
A beer?
Well, yes, seeing as how it's good for the milk and all.
We settled in, the conversation was thin, morbid really,
The things they had done to her children:
Her first born bull-calf penned up and slaughtered;
Her Bonnie forced to breed too young,
They had no childhood, don't you see,
She rolled her deep black eyes,
I'll tell you what they think I am,
A factory, that's what,
The things I could tell you about teat pain,
It's a matter of attitude, you can trust me on that one,
The grass keeps growing,
One endures.

Madigan waltz

Did you say Santa Fe?
Those long fields of sky between the Rio and the road,
Cherries? Rutabagas? Of course, I'd heard about
outlaws and in-laws,
Mountains, the Blood of The Christ,
box canyons, caves, like that,
You know. Oh I know you know,
Roosters at dawn; at sunset, quince.
Bathing in arsenic, modest men with such a variety of penises,
The raves, dirt streets, dirt houses. It's that, isn't it? Cosy mud.
Ask your daughter if you don't believe me, she'll tell you. Earth.
How can you help but smile when you pass those polished
cement-floored boutiques?
Forgive me a wink. So somewhere else.
The book stores lined with conversations,
Smoking, as mundane here as anywhere but more compelling,
more *del terra*, wouldn't you say?
Those murmuring bones around the cathedral, for example,
You do hear them, don't you, Pinecone?
I'm counting on you to come through,
just this once for me and Rose de Lima. Pretty please.
The March winds are always raw.
Crossing the Plaza, just steps away from those woman-scented
blooms, the image that comes to mind:
Mountains and in the *arroyos*,
Aspens.

Sun blowing sideways
in Santa Fe

Cold wind in the Plaza,
Sunlight blown sideways,
Up against the Governor's Palace,
Shivering women in blankets selling silver,
Too early still for customers,
Billy the Kid languishes in his basement cell,
Upstairs "The Collected Works" sells
Six different books about his life and death,
But not a single copy of Lew Wallace's Ben Hur,
Governor Wallace, that is, the man who wouldn't save him.
Down at the Bijou, the Dalai Lama rises smiling
Again and again above his country's sorrow,
Soon the shops will open, fill with tourists,
The women draw their blankets across their faces,
The sunlight blows sideways against my shadow,
Sweeping it into the fir trees
And frozen ground of the Cathedral,
I lie there gazing at the mountain,
As satisfied as pine needles
That things are as they are.

It was me who built the wall

I built a wall of 721 concrete blocks, each 16 x 8 x 8 inches,
Stuccoed it, set in tiles, hung an ancient bell,
hammered together gates of beaten wood and locked it.
The coyotes watched from the shadows every day
with their yellow eyes,
Every night they yipped and howled outlandish threats,
How they would devour first the cat and then the baby,
How they would gnaw off our feet while we slept
and piss on the furniture too,
"Good walls make bad neighbors," they barked,
Quoting Robert Frost's mongrel.
When I hit the five foot level I yelled back,
"Jump over that, you punks."
But the trees didn't like the wall either,
"We're here only for you to admire," they whispered,
"We live for your praises. Why do you wall beauty out?"
A rogue cactus and a cat's claw bush
took up the chorus,
And I couldn't sleep for their taunts.
Even some of the rocks grumbled
that I had betrayed them.
The birds, finches and jays together,
sat on the rising wall and chatted, as they do,
about freedom. Infuriating.
But I had spent so much time and energy on it,
dreaming about the Gates of Heaven
and comparing them to my gates
I couldn't let it go.
In the end I agreed to put openings in it,
to swing the gates back on their hinges.
The trees said it wasn't perfect,

but they'd live with it if I'd sing to them at dawn,
The day it was finished,
coyotes came at sunset and chased the cat to the top of the wall,
they rang the bell, pulling the rope with their shining teeth
and carried off the baby's clothes from the clothesline.
The rocks remain stoic and unmoved to this day,
and the cat's claw bush scratches me every chance it gets.

Lunar eclipse

Mars bleeds into sunset,
And the sky fills up with portents.
In the north a comet shreds itself against the twilight,
A dark sun cackles below the horizon,
and the moon, that light maddened bitch, wheels into eclipse.
In the forest, a juniper sticks out a root
to trip anyone who passes,
"This is the end," she glowers pulling in her shadows close.

Coyotes unwrap the charts of heaven they had not yet sung
and tear through the blazing bushes chanting like monks.
In the night garden, silence hangs by her neck in a noose,
Dreams reel by on the walls of the air,
And the grass, o the blades of bloody grass, shriek
As though they are the final conquerors.

The moon's best night yet

The longest night in a century,
Black except the moon –
knowing a big break when she sees one –
Lifts her billowy skirts, swings close, closer, closest,
And flings it in earth's old rogue's face.
Brother Sun, caged on the other side of the world,
burns against the bars,
While Luna frolics above the ooohing and ahhhing of the rocks,
Cliffs, inflamed by her dance, tremble and weep waterfalls,
Evergreen forests pale at a glimpse of her bosom,
While the wolves run on,
Until dawn throws back the covers
And catches the whole tumbling beauty of it
Flagrante delicti.

Moors still live in southern Spain

When the carob tree sings the old songs,
The crescent moon pins up her silken robes
To dance with midnight,
The oleander strums a few chords
On the strings of the brook,
And the wanton fig throws back
Her dark and dewy leaves
To show the bashful olive her pink fruit.

In one of the ancient white houses
A woman sighs and turns away,
A man closes the door softly,
And begins to walk down the muffled road,
The air smells of jasmine,
Somewhere a zither plays,
Before he reaches home
He has fallen in love —
With the moon.

A morning after
New Year's Eve

A yellow moon growls down on St Germain
one last time
Frightening the self-satisfied apartments
out of their smug dreams,
The boulevard empties itself of darkness
like a spent lover,
As a new sun, full of hope and vigor,
Whispers again in all the pink ears
of the Pantheon,
The Luxembourg Garden stretches herself
and scratches those places
Where the statues of thinkers and artists
have been itching like fleas all night —
As though famous people
were the most irritating of all.

*S*pirit

Mind and body served me well enough for years. Then one day, without warning, the world of the spirit opened to me, a vast and shining secret continent. Here was a new way of seeing, a fresh way of being. Consciousness heightened, ignorance lightened. Oneness with others and with the cosmos waited in the heart to be unwrapped like a gift. Silence had wings. I had always believed we each had the power within us to change our lives and here, much to my astonishment, my life had been changed in a way I could never have imagined.

For a long time I was able to coast along on the power and depth of that first glimpse. Gradually, though, the details, the flotsam and jetsam, accumulated and began to clog the river of light. Faith and doubt danced together in my dreams. Joy and sorrow sat down with me for breakfast and argued until the eggs were cold and the coffee grew bitter. What they eventually agreed on was that what had been given by grace could be sustained by choice. Better joy than sorrow; better kindness than uncaring; better hope than despair; better light than darkness; better gratitude than bitterness; and that seeking is only another way of finding.

Old vessels buried

The red earth opens near Magdelena,
Unclasps the moon
To walk on fire, barefoot,
Over San Francisco's burning peaks.
Anasazi pot shards vibrate in the ground like skulls,
As though will or meditation could bring back time.
An old wind rushes between the zig-zag lines
Black, white, black, white, black

You feel the painter's hand tremble against your eyelids,
What is death like?
You hold your own life up to the light
And ask if it is beautiful.

Trees we love and ignore

Suppose we could see beauty bare,
stripped down, essential,
fresh and always there?

A man sits in a garden
troubled by his life
and other lives.
A small wind stirs in the leaves of a sycamore,
And in that breathing he sees that
there has always been an opening,
a way through,
And wonders what part of him it is
That makes him blind.

Why I am Tibetan

When I was nine, I thought Tibet
Was an impossible place on some other planet,
As unreachable as Pluto.
Still, snow leopards crossed my path,
Boys, heavier than me, rose on dragon kites
Over plunging gorges.
I drank yak milk in limestone caves,
And never thought of God or China.
Prayer wheels spun dizzy in the thin air,
Flags sent chants up the thermals like crows into heaven,
Blue black against the staggering height of sky.
When I first saw a picture of the Potalah,
I knew it was bigger and better
Than the Empire State Building,
It seemed the safest place in the universe,
Something like love that could never change.
Now I know better what prayer and love can do,
How they work from the inside out,
Slowly with such power,
The way wind and water will one day
Flatten the Himalayas.

Dick's magic hat

One night while dreaming in his bed,
Dick dreams a buzzing in his head,
He throws it in his Crazy Cap,
Slips down to Honeyland instead,
Doffs his chapeau to honey bees,
And sailors of the Seven Seas,
Who drowning let their thinking rage,
High above them in the waves,
And give their bodies to the tides,
And settle in to soulful lives,
That await them on the other side.

Embroidered with the sun and moon,
That Crazy Cap, brocaded boon,
Drop your thoughts into the hat,
They disappear in nothing flat,
And what is left inside your head,
Slips down to Honeyland instead,
Slips down to Honeyland instead.

Adobe

OK, Light of my life, it's like this: Build on rock –
but build of sand.
Sand and earth. And heaven too. This Eden cool in summer,
snug in winter.
This air you make sweet by moving through. Oh, I remember
temptation. What of it?
It's what made us forgiving. No? Each block weighs 50 pounds.
Fifty bricks a day. That's a ton and a half to heft – plus the mortar
to raise the walls of one small house in the desert.
You could say in the wilderness.
You could say clay and wattles.
You could say forty years meandering
before we could set stone on stone.
Here's a secret: nothing is simple. Or everything is simple.
So many live their lives backwards.

The birds think we're dangerous – except at feeding time,
Spring is so late the lizards sleep into April. So dry no turtles sing.
We, on the other hand, sleep the sleep of children,
Do we not? Chaste. Pure as stars in each others arms.
I saw your body in the clouds long after midnight,
round and full of breath.
And the sound of the sea washing against a shore I've never visited.
This morning a mosque, itself a kind of tree, grew out of the
mud beyond the junipers. Mud-made. Domed. Minueted.
Blue tiled. You whispered: "God and leaves."
This evening monks will come from another country to rest their
backs against the massive wall.
Listen. Those songs we used to sing? It's the sky who sings them now.
Lean back, my sweetest. Feel my hands.
How rough they've become with praying.

On a day that starts badly

By chance, in the morning paper,
on a day that starts badly,
A print of an old Chinese painting,
called "Serenity and Wind."

Under a bend of trees,
a man without age
fishes quietly.

His life passes
on the surface
of a delicate pond.

The world comes and goes
in the carps' velvet eyes.

The charms of the world — Uxmal

Another crazy tourist
running up the so-steep narrow stairs
of the Temple of the White Dwarf,
O God,
Oh look at me.

And now the blood, the old stories,
Fear the colour of sunset,
The body devoured by axes and stars
Wrung by pythons,
While the old ones watch
from the Pleiades
and Mars.

O elegance, O beauty, O Uxmal!

Weep with me my jaguar-friend
for this fleeting life.
How long will we lie together dead?
How long will this world go on without us?
Where now must we hunt for God?

Now I have a stone garden

Now I have a stone garden
The grass never thrived
It made me feel inadequate
Like someone in a tv commerical
Whose soul depended
On the quality of the front lawn.
Now I feel like a Zen master
Before enlightenment: rake stones
After enlightenment: rake stones.